LET'S PLAY TAG!

Read the Page

Read the Story

Game

Yes   No

Repeat

Stop

INTERNET CONNECTION REQUIRED FOR AUDIO DOWNLOAD.

To use this book with the Tag™ Reader you must download audio from the LeapFrog® Connect Application.
The LeapFrog Connect Application can be installed from the CD provided with your Tag Reader or at leapfrog.com/tag.

FINDING DRAGO

Adapted by Tracey West

One day, strange cards fell from the sky.
The cards fell all over the world.

Dan and his friends used the cards to make up a game.

They called the game Bakugan.

They called themselves the Bakugan Battle Brawlers.

Each card held a Bakugan inside.

The Bakugan came to life when the card was thrown down.

Brawlers battled using their Bakugan.

Dan loved to battle whenever he could.

One day, he ran to the park after school.

It was time for a Bakugan brawl!

Shuji was ready to brawl with Dan.

"You think you are pretty good," Shuji said.

"Let's find out how good you really are."

Dan battled Shuji.

He beat all of Shuji's Bakugan!

 Dan's battle was over. But another battle was going on.

This battle was in a place called Vestroia.

Vestroia is the home of all the Bakugan.

Naga, a Dragonoid Bakugan, lived in Vestroia.

He wanted all the power for himself.

He did not care how he got it.

Drago tried to stop Naga.

"Wait!" Drago yelled. "You will destroy us all!"

Naga did not listen. He flew to the Silent Core, the place that held all the negative power in Vestroia.

The next day, Dan ran into Shuji again.

"I want a rematch!" Shuji said.

"So you like losing?" Dan asked.

"Just zip it!" Shuji said. "Let's brawl!"

"Bakugan Brawl!" Shuji yelled.

He threw a Bakugan onto the field.

It turned into a Darkus Juggernoid.

It looked like a big, bad turtle.

Then it was Dan's turn. "Bakugan Brawl!" he yelled.
He threw out a Pyrus Saurus. It looked like a red dinosaur.

Shuji tossed out a new Bakugan to take care of Saurus.

Darkus Stinglash looked creepy!

It had a scorpion's body and a human face.

Stinglash had a lot of power—330 Gs.

Dan had to give Saurus more power.

He used a Gate Card. Now Saurus had 310 Gs.

It was not enough. Stinglash battled Saurus.

Stinglash won!

While the boys battled, Naga was still after more power. He found the Silent Core. The energy made him feel strong. "More! More! Feel the power!" Naga yelled.

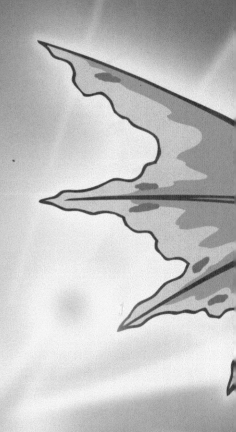

Meanwhile, Dan was still battling Shuji. He looked up in the sky.

He could see the hole between the worlds.

He saw Drago flying through waves of fire.

"That was weird!" Dan said.

Dan kept on battling. Shuji used Stinglash again.

Dan threw out a Pyrus Serpenoid.

But the big snake did not have enough power to beat Stinglash.

Dan used a card called Quartet Battle.

Now two more Bakugan could join the brawl.

But something strange happened. The card began to glow.

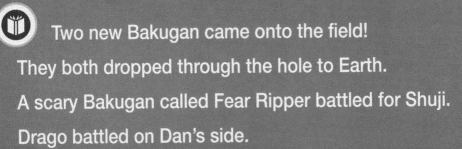 Two new Bakugan came onto the field!

They both dropped through the hole to Earth.

A scary Bakugan called Fear Ripper battled for Shuji.

Drago battled on Dan's side.

"Come to your senses!" Drago yelled to Fear Ripper.

"Snap out of it! We can stop this fight."

But Fear Ripper did not listen. He kept fighting.

Drago did not want to fight Fear Ripper.

But he had no choice.

"Boosted Dragon!" Drago yelled.

He shot a big ball of fire from his mouth.

The fireball took down Fear Ripper!

Dan was shocked. The Dragonoid on the field was talking!

His Bakugan had never talked before.

Drago and Fear Ripper turned into Bakugan balls. "I lost again!" Shuji wailed. Dan looked at the Bakugan. "Did you really talk?" he asked. "Hmm. Since you are a Dragonoid, I will name you Drago."

Dan ran home. He talked to his friends on his computer.

"You will not believe this," he told them.

"I heard my Bakugan talk today!"

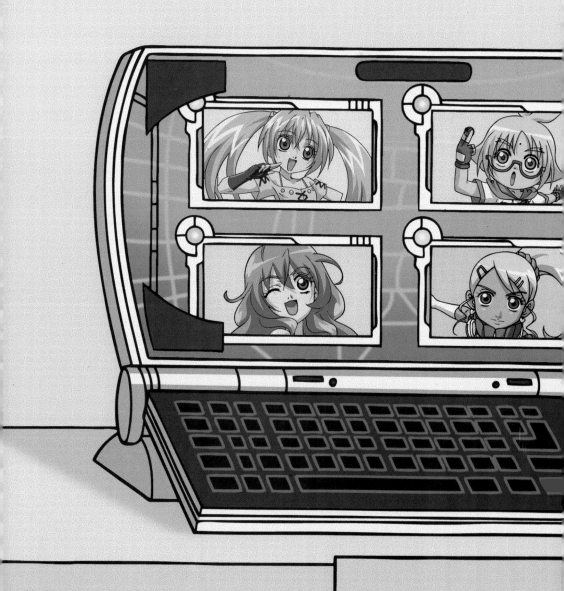

"Me too!" said his friend Runo.

Dan looked down at Drago. "Maybe the Bakugan world has more to it than we thought!" Dan said.